GW00864999

Howard Colyer was born near Brixton Hill in Lo

Gregory Gun is devoted to his job and he is made redundant. And then he struggles. He tries to cope and he fights against his own character; but finally he shuts himself away and becomes a hermit in London, and lives a strange and secret life.

Gregory Gun

Howard Colyer

Arial 12

ISBN 978-1-84728-944-5

Copyright © 2006 by Howard Colyer. All rights reserved.

Lulu North Carolina USA

Gregory Gun looked through the grimy windows and watched the builders arrive in the street below. They assembled gradually, coming in ones and twos, and stood about, and chatted and smoked. Only one man sat alone, occupied with a crossword. And although Gregory was eager to know which one it was, he could only tell it was in a broadsheet newspaper. He hoped that when the builder got up he would open and refold it. But when a man arrived in a tie and tweed jacket, the builder slipped the paper at once into his knapsack. Left uncertain Gregory felt frustrated and sad.

Yet he did not linger over his feelings, but went out of the main office on the second storey to the smaller room which adjoined it, and which led to the stairs. He checked to see if the furniture was in the right place; giving it one last shove to satisfy himself.

He had jammed five desks together, so that they formed a solid block between the door onto the landing and the opposite wall. The door was also locked, and pinned to its frame by a dozen three inch nails. Even with sledge hammers, Gregory thought, the builders would take a few minutes to break their way in. Then they would have to demolish the inner door. Gregory was as secure as he could be in the circumstances.

He was glad that the end would come in the place where he had lived more than in any other. It seemed fitting to him, though he accepted that to many it might seem odd. This floor had been his domain: two offices, six staff and their own kitchen and toilets. For eleven years he had presided there. Now he was alone. Yet the builders were still in the street, and so for a little longer he felt as if he were in control.

It was no novelty for Gregory to be in charge in the building, even though he had only ever been deputy manager. He had concentrated on running the branch, thus leaving the managers he had served under free to concentrate on customers, regional meetings, and other such activities which had kept them away from daily concerns.

Gregory had always preferred administration. It had suited his orderly nature. But the merit of his character had become a burden to him when he had been confronted with a request for a large and complicated loan. Straightforward mortgages and overdrafts never troubled Gregory, but he was afraid of commercial accounts. And as he worked in the Holborn branch it was a definite handicap, but one he owned to. He was often told that a certain diffidence was only natural when faced with a complicated proposal; but Gregory was never able to bear the prospect of failing the bank. He was assured that all managers made mistakes, and that a certain percentage of loans always became bad debts: but this troubled Gregory. And much that happened during the last ten years at the branch was consequently painful for him; and pushed him further towards the humdrum side of banking.

Gregory saw himself as a deputy manager's deputy manager; though he never expressed himself in these terms to others. He was offered suburban branches to run but declined them. He never saw his job as a step leading upwards: he was happy to take second place. He regarded his role as one of shielding the branch manager from distractions so that he could devote himself to financial decisions. If the managers he served under were profligate with the bank's money it was not because they were troubled by matters of routine. Gregory was painstakingly thorough, and the branch was a model of regulated commerce. He knew he was mocked for his pedantic ways, and he knew he could be very irritating; but he also knew he was respected.

Nineteen of Gregory's thirty-four years in the bank were spent in the Holborn branch. After he was transferred there from Fleet Street in 1974 he never attempted to leave. For Gregory it seemed like his true home.

Gregory's other home was in Bromley. It was a feature of his life that was even more fixed than his job, for he never moved. His parents started to pay the mortgage on the house while it was being built in 1930. It was made habitable just in time for their first child, April, to be born there; and ten years later Gregory arrived during an air raid. Which was something his mother told him countless times, citing his violent birth as an explanation for everything he did, or didn't do, which she found unusual.

His mother died of cancer when Gregory was twenty, after a short illness. Soon afterwards Gregory's father was also found to have cancer, but he survived for another six years. Gregory and his sister stayed in the house, caring for him: a dutiful bachelor and spinster.

April was an attractive woman, but nervous and sickly. She was troubled by a bad stomach and palpitations, which occasionally at night she mistook for a heart attack. She would cry out, 'Gregory, Gregory, I'm dying!' And she would bang on the wall with a strength which belied her fear.

Gregory was certain that her illnesses were psychosomatic, but he was also certain that her suffering was real; and as they grew older his private life came to revolve around his sister's well-being. They spent most of their weekends together, and all of their holidays: every spring Gregory drove her to Devon, and every autumn to Normandy.

His sister was also the cause of Gregory remaining a bachelor. He was hardly a philanderer, but there were two women in his life who he thought he could marry, both of whom he worked with at Holborn.

Hilary was the first of these. He had met her briefly at Fleet Street before he was transferred, and five years later she also moved to Holborn. Hilary was given the counter post beside Gregory's and they discovered a joint passion for crosswords. This was during the year in which The Times wasn't published, and he had resorted to The Daily Telegraph, and she to The Guardian. In the morning they worked on his paper, and in the afternoon hers. Then they started having their lunches together in the Princess Louise. And one evening after work they had kissed in Sicilian Avenue.

They were lovers for six months, until April's hatred finished their affair. She had hated Hilary before she met her, and more so after Hilary visited the Guns' house one Sunday for lunch. After this confrontation he accepted that his sister and Hilary would never be able to live together; and also that he couldn't abandon April.

He told Hilary this while they were having a drink in the Duke of Wellington. She had said nothing for five minutes, during which Gregory had apologised in a tumble of half sentences. Then she asked him if he were really choosing his sister in preference to his girlfriend; and he said, 'Yes'. Later that evening Hilary wrote her resignation letter to the bank.

Gregory tried to get her to stay, but she said she was too unhappy to continue working with him. Consequently he was doubly guilty. At her leaving drink he had only one pint before saying a hurried good-bye. Then he wandered off towards Victoria, but only walked half a mile before he stopped to cry on a bench in Soho Square. His pain though didn't change his conviction that duty came before love.

Two and a half years later a secretary called Jane started working in the branch. She was a vivacious woman who didn't like crosswords, but to Gregory's amazement started flirting with him. They had lunch together, and Gregory was flattered to discover that he amused her. Briefly forgetting his conviction he started seeing Jane in the evenings, until April reared her shapely head and objected. Like Hilary, Jane was amazed by Gregory's choice; unlike her predecessor though she phlegmatically continued with her life.

This second affair ended the day before Gregory was promoted to deputy manager, and he had not been blind to the symbolism. Not only did Gregory think it wrong for someone in authority to pursue his female staff, he also saw that for him it was futile. April would not accept any woman as his wife, therefore he resolved to remain single. He buried his emotional needs under the extra work he did to excel in his new position.

And with a timing which seemed to justify her jealousy, April was diagnosed as having cancer. Years of hypochondria had not saved her from the family disease. April's illness followed the slow wasting pattern of her father's, and during her gradual death she became ever more tyrannical with her brother. Who not only became more browbeaten, but also more anxious, as every new mark and bump on his own body suggested the onset of cancer. However despite his panicky visits to Bromley Hospital there remained a kernel of certainty in Gregory's mind, that death would first isolate him and then take him.

He was right. He endured good health during the long years of April's decline, and not a week went by without her reproaching him for his good fortune. Understandably her death was a relief to Gregory, though it was also a loss. He didn't like her, but he loved her. Without April there was only work, and his life felt lopsided. However the bank moved to end this imbalance. It marked the Holborn branch for closure.

Gregory argued fiercely against this. He sent memo after memo proclaiming the necessity of the branch; but he convinced no one who mattered. For the first time in his life he attended a union meeting, where he declared, 'A bank without branches is like a navy without ships;' and he won the applause of those who feared for their jobs. However all his efforts were futile. The closure of the Holborn branch was not even delayed by a day. The sole effect of his campaign was to end any doubt about his unsuitability for the new style of bank envisaged by its senior managers. They declared Gregory redundant.

The change did not leave him impoverished. The bank was generous with those it discarded, and Gregory was not poor. His house was worth £200,000; he had never had to pay rent or a mortgage, and he had no expensive habits. Every month of his career he had saved. When his colleagues asked him what he was going to do he was able to say, 'At least there won't be any shortage of money.' And these few words became his stock defence. At the farewell dinner in My Old Dutch he ended up repeating them softly, almost to himself, in a drunken stupor; until a clerk who lived in Chiselhurst had the kindness to lead him away, and find them both a taxi.

Gregory spent the next two days in his dressing gown and pyjamas. It was only on the following Monday that he felt physically better, and completely lost; and then he began his days of emptiness.

On that first workless Monday he left the house at his usual time and took the usual short walk to the newsagent's and purchased The Times – and a pint of milk. After returning home and making tea, he started on the Cryptic crossword, and felt chastised on reading the first clue: 1 ACROSS, 'Confess about wine being terrible (8).' For he had increasingly come to see crossword clues as having personal significance.

On completing the Cryptic he moved on to the Quick; and became slightly happier through being able to solve the crossword in the order in which the clues were given.   Until he found it finished with, 19 DOWN, 'Drab and joyless (6).'

Then he went shopping, and bought The Daily Telegraph and Evening Standard. Once home he put his shopping away and sat down at the kitchen table with the newspapers. He cut out their four crosswords and meandered between them until a little before five o'clock. Then for the rest of the day he despaired.

The next morning he tried to rally himself and start life afresh, 'Come on Gregory, no self-pity please, you were born in an air raid after all.'

He resolved to be busy and cheerful; though he was immediately defeated by the problem of being busy without work. To be cheerful he decided to go to a pub every lunchtime. And in the weeks that followed he even talked to strangers and barmaids.   But whichever pub he went to, and whoever he talked to, he felt himself to be a bore. He tried not to discuss the bank but his conversation always strayed that way; and when he wasn't talking about the job he had lost he fell to discussing crosswords and cancer.

So he soon gave up pubs and took to eating in restaurants, and was careful to bother no one with his talk. Instead he tried to enliven himself by a series of short holidays; but without April's needs and company the trips seemed too obviously a way of killing time. All they did was make him look forward to going home; but when he was there he wanted to go away.

For it did not seem right to Gregory that he should live at home by himself. He felt that it was only his house legally, that in truth it belonged still to his parents and sister. Beyond his own room he had never had any say in domestic matters. His idea of the essence of the house was so entwined with memories of his dead family that he didn't feel they had properly gone. This made him very cautious: he changed nothing, but only made repairs. And he stopped going in the other bedrooms, except once a week to hoover and dust. More frequent incursions would have seemed intrusive.

This sense of respect was not a result of Gregory's redundancy, but it weighed upon him now he had no office to go to; and the longer he was unemployed the more he felt he was living in a tomb.

Naturally as it was his family's tomb he could not sell it. Though it did occur to Gregory that if he had a wife there with him then the atmosphere might change; and for other reasons the idea of a wife was appealing. He accepted that as he was only fifty-four and comfortably wealthy he should be able to find a woman who would marry him. Yet the idea merely seemed an abstract possibility: he could imagine a man as old and as rich as himself getting married, but only if that man were not Gregory Gun. He doubted he had been a bachelor by nature, but long practice had brought him to a state of withdrawal from which he could not even escape in his imagination. The hope of a woman had died.

Gregory made an attempt to keep in touch with his ex-colleagues, but these efforts proved short lived. On the last occasion on which he met any of them he had a drink with two of the assistant managers. Both of whom had volunteered for redundancy. They looked very different in their sweatshirts and jeans from how he remembered them; and Gregory felt alien in his blazer and carefully pressed woollen trousers. One of the men was now a decorator, and the other worked in a warehouse. Both professed to be happy; neither regretted the change; and neither seemed worried by the prospect of more change. Gregory thought they were wrong to be happy. For though he had been abandoned by the bank, he was still loyal to what he had been.

If Gregory had needed money to live his position would have been different; but without the threat of poverty he was incapable of helping himself. He could not find the sort of work he wanted – employment agencies just told him to go away – and he was too rich to stomach anything strange. Gregory wanted a position of middling authority in a commercial hierarchy, and none were available for anyone like him.

Gregory's days became exceedingly long. He found himself dragging out whatever he did; and it was rare for half-an-hour to go by without him looking at his watch and regretting how little time had passed.

With the aid of sleeping tablets he managed to escape his boredom at about nine o'clock every night. This meant he was generally awake by four, but he was content to lie in bed and watch the dawn arrive. It was his most pleasant activity of the day: the world was very quiet then and his loneliness not so apparent; and he never feared that his parents or April would visit him at sunrise.

At about eight o'clock he would have breakfast and complete the Cryptic crossword in The Times; then he would slowly do his chores so that they would last all morning. He would go out for lunch, and with the aid of a book take two hours over a light meal. Depending on the weather, in the afternoons he would either sit in Bromley Library, or amble about the streets and parks. In the evenings he ate a sandwich, completed the Quick crossword, and struggled all the while against taking his sleeping draught too early.

On most days the height of his sociability was to feed the pigeons. On seeing him approach across the Common they would form a swirling flock, which would orbit Gregory until he reached a certain tree and then descend. The experience reminded him of arriving at work with the door keys. Unlike at work though he would soon wander away.

Gregory envied the pigeons. He even envied the ants he sometimes watched. They were perpetually busy: all of them. There did not seem to be a single redundant ant, nor an abandoned nest. Years before Gregory had read somewhere that man is not capable of achieving even an animal level of happiness. He had not thought anything of the idea at the time; it had looked as if it were a striking, but bogus generalisation. Now Gregory felt himself to be outmatched by the joys of insects.

He realised this while watching a crack in the earth which served as a gateway to a nest. For the next ten minutes Gregory stamped about furiously and ground his heels until the crack was closed. He didn't bother to eat that evening but swallowed his tablets at six o'clock. On waking up at one a.m. he decided he would return to the branch.

Gregory had resolved never to go back to Holborn, but he could keep away no longer. He did not expect to gain anything from the trip; indeed he feared that the sight of the branch converted to a pub or something would cause him considerable pain. Yet he felt compelled to go. Having made his decision he couldn't get back to sleep, so he got up, had a bath and dressed as if he were going to work. Gregory reached Bromley South station twenty minutes before the first train of the day. To keep warm and calm he walked three times up and down the full length of the platform. He tried to read on the way to Victoria but he couldn't. He travelled two stops on the tube to Oxford Circus, changed, then two more stops and he was at Holborn.

Gregory stood outside the branch at dawn. He did not feel as miserable as he had expected; largely he thought because almost nothing seemed to have been done in his absence. The front door had a large padlock on it; and the counter had gone, but judging by what else he could see through the windows the branch was not being refurbished.

He walked round to the back. The door there was not padlocked, and the lock did not appear to have been changed. Gregory ran the little finger of his right hand along the door handle, and looked at the grime. He walked away, cleaning his little finger with his handkerchief. He walked as far as Russell Square, circled it, and returned. He studied the back door again. Then he headed off towards Covent Garden. He bought The Times in a newsagent's in Drury Lane, and stopped in Russell Street for breakfast at Café Valerie. There he didn't read his newspaper or attempt the crosswords, but sat with his mind half lost in memories and half in an idea for the next day.

When the branch closed Gregory had not returned his set of keys. He had not held on to these by accident, but as solid proof of the trust he had enjoyed.

On the train the next morning he thought he might be violating that trust by what he intended to do. He was too excited though to stop. Again he reached the branch at dawn and peered through the windows. There was nobody within and he hurried to the back door. He took out a can of WD40 from his briefcase and sprayed the lock. He inserted the key, but it stuck. He took it out, and put it back in, wiggled it, and with a twist made it turn.

Gregory stepped into the bottom of the stairwell. It was cold and damp. The lights didn't work, but before he could find his torch he heard footsteps in the alley and shut the door. The one spot of light was the keyhole and Gregory managed to lock himself in. The footsteps didn't approach but even so Gregory remained rigid for a couple of minutes; then he called himself a, 'panicky old fool,' and pulled his torch out from the sleeve on the side of his bag.

He undid the iron grill at the bottom of the steps and followed his torch beam up to the first floor. The cupboards had been emptied and the desks cleared, and the furniture had been left askew; but it was still recognisable as the main office of the Holborn branch.

For a few minutes Gregory looked about him. Then he tidied the chairs. As he did so he thought about the people who had worked there, then he thought about their predecessors in their jobs. He thought about the succession of clerks who had worked there for nineteen years – but more than any other he thought of Hilary.

He explored every room. Each had been left like the main office. Gregory returned to it and adjusted one of the blinds so that he could look down to the road without being seen. Dawn was giving way to morning and Holborn was getting busier. He wondered how long it would be until another company moved in to the empty building. Holborn though seemed to be in decline. Pearl Assurance had left and their offices were empty, and other buildings were empty too. Gregory didn't understand what was wrong with the street.

He turned away from the window and walked to the stairs. He paused for a few seconds, then went up to his old office on the second floor. His desk was still there but it had been pushed against a wall, and his chair stood forlorn in the middle of the room. Gregory pulled them back to their rightful places. He wiped the dust away as best he could with a loose bit of carpet from the kitchen. Then he resumed his place: he took off his overcoat and sat at his desk in his suit. Gregory remained there for an hour, held fast under a flood of memories.

He might have remained there much longer if he had not been brought back to the present by a siren. 'The police are here!' he thought; then, with relief, he realised it was an ambulance. Gregory went to the window and watched it struggle through the traffic. He shivered. Suddenly aware of how cold he had become he put on his coat and decided to leave. Going outside though was a challenge, because he was certain that somebody would be in the alley when he opened the door. Yet he could only leave unseen if he waited until night. Gregory told himself to pretend that he was a surveyor from the Buildings Department of the bank, and that he had been inspecting the property.

Gregory walked to and fro saying, 'You're a surveyor, you're a surveyor, you're a surveyor.' He repeated the words all the way down the stairs; and despite the passing commuters he unlocked and locked the door boldly. He even had the self-possession to give the door a firm tug before walking away. Though it was only after he rounded the corner and crossed the road that he stopped repeating his lie.

He made his way to Café Valerie. Where he celebrated with a smoked salmon breakfast. 'Perhaps I should become a thief,' he joked to himself in his glee. But beneath his excitement at his escapade there was a sense of relief. Gregory had found a source of calm: a refuge.

On his way to the branch he had thought about throwing his keys into the Thames after his visit. He had envisaged standing on the Embankment and watching them drop to the water and vanish in an instant. Now he was tempted to go back again. He told himself that it had to be his last visit or he risked being caught. For despite Holborn's decay he was convinced the building would be sold. This fear spurred him to return quickly. When he left the café he was minded to go back during the next week. By the time he reached Bromley he had decided to go the next day.

Gregory's second visit followed the pattern of his first. On his third visit he bought a copy of The Times before he reached the branch, and did the Cryptic crossword by torchlight at his desk. Later that morning he had a spare set of keys cut. For a fortnight he went to the branch on Tuesdays and Thursdays. Then he went every day.

One morning he used the toilet which adjoined his office. To his surprise he thought he heard the main tank fill up. He hurried up the stairs to the top landing but by the time he got there the noise had stopped. He went down and flushed the toilet again and ran the taps. When he got back to the landing he could hear the peculiar gurgle in the loft which had permeated the upper half of the building during much of the working day. Gregory called himself an idiot for not having tested the taps before. He had assumed that the water would have been cut off at the same time as the electricity. Obviously it hadn't.

Later, after breakfast, he went to the Black's camping shop by Chancery Lane underground station. He bought a small stove, a dozen gas canisters, a kettle and a tin mug. In Gray's Inn Road he bought tea, milk and sugar; and, in a moment of inspiration, butter and bread. Then he returned to Black's and bought a plastic plate and a lightweight set of cutlery.

Gregory did not go directly back to the branch but walked about in Lincoln's Inn Fields. Excited by his idea he hadn't considered the dangers of returning to the office in daylight. However as the alternative was to take everything to Bromley, then back the next day, he decided to make the attempt. He would walk along the alley, and if no one was about he would go in, otherwise he would go home: the alley was deserted and Gregory regained the branch.

He put the stove on the table of the second floor kitchen, and the kettle on the stove. He made tea, and emptied the kettle and hung it on a hook. Then he forked a slice of bread and moved it about the flame. His buttered toast tasted beautiful. Gregory spent the afternoon in the branch and went home during the rush hour.

With the advent of tea making Gregory's routine changed. Instead of going home after breakfast he went for a short walk, and then returned to the branch. Nearly all of his time there he spent in his old office. Occasionally he would venture to the first or third floors, but the ground floor he hardly visited due to his fear of being seen. However he did take one liberty there. For though he had never aspired to be a branch manager, he had long coveted a branch manager's chair. It was far more sumptuous than the chairs allowed to the lower grades: it was wide, tall, deeply padded, and its back could be let down to make it ripe for the afternoon nap.

Fearing that he would injure himself if he tried to lift it up to the second floor in a day, Gregory worked the chair up one flight of stairs each morning. Starting on a Tuesday he finished on a Friday. After a post-breakfast stroll in Bloomsbury, and a toasted lunch and a crossword, he took possession of his chair in the afternoon. He re-lit the gas stove, wrapped himself in his overcoat, sat down, and lowered the chair's back as far as it would go.

Due to his early start to the day during the week Gregory was generally tired on a Friday, and had expected to fall asleep. Instead he thought about the course of his life: about the odd turn it had taken and the uncertainty of what lay ahead. It was not a happy subject and only slowly did his thoughts become dreams; and they too were unhappy.

He woke with a start at eight o'clock. The stove had gone out, it was dark, and he was chilled. Disappointed in his luxury he hurried home.

The next week he bought a second, bigger gas stove, and a sleeping bag. This had zips at the shoulders, as well as in the middle, thus allowing its occupant's arms to come out. Snug now Gregory was able to read before he dozed. However as he usually woke up after dark he feared the light from the stoves might be noticed outside. Therefore he kept the blinds shut. And as his torch quickly drained batteries Gregory bought a large number of candles; and so read and slept in a circle of flames, within a circle of shadows.

Every evening he would stay in the manager's chair until seven o'clock. Then he would tidy up and set off for Bromley. This habit lasted until one Friday night when he felt disinclined to open his sleeping bag, scrape clean the candle holders, and put everything away. So he granted himself an extra hour.

At eight o'clock he thought seriously about going home, but he was still in his chair at eight-thirty. At nine o'clock he decided he would get up at five past, and made a similar resolution at ten o'clock. At eleven o'clock he gave in and accepted he would stay.

Having come to this conclusion though he failed to get back to sleep. Instead he found himself listening to the street get quieter and quieter. Until eventually there was just the sound of a car passing by every ten minutes or so, and the intimidating laughter of a few drunken groups drifting away from the West End. He wondered if any one would try and break in and what they would do to him if they did. He assumed he would be savagely beaten: he saw himself being kicked about his office to the chant of 'Weirdo!' But he was left to be afraid in peace.

With the dawn came a small sense of triumph, and he smiled at his fears as he restored his office to order. His happiness was diminished though when he set off for Bromley, unshaven and in clothes he had worn for a day.

Despite his lack of sleep Gregory was also awake for most of Saturday night. He lay in bed uneasy and tempted, in the room in which he had been born, and which had been his all his life. Again he got up at dawn; and washed and dressed, and went for a walk along his old route on Bromley Common.

Gregory had forgotten about the pigeons and was surprised when they flocked about him. He stood and looked at them and they looked at him, but he had brought nothing for their breakfast.

Surrounded by a cooing, disconsolate mob he returned home.

He started to pack. As he did so he kept asking, 'Gregory, what are you doing?' But he ignored the question and carried on. When he had filled two large suitcases and a shoulder bag he called for a taxi to take him to Paddington Station. He told the driver he was going to Cardiff to visit a friend. From Paddington he took a taxi to Holborn; and told the driver he had arrived from Cardiff, and that he was going to meet a friend in a pub before going on to Folkestone. Gregory had no idea as to who would try and trace his movements, but he felt he had to be devious.

After being dropped outside the Princess Louise Gregory rummaged in his shoulder bag until the taxi had disappeared. Then he hobbled along the empty street to the branch. He took his bags up to his office one at a time, and made tea in his new home. Despite his fears of Friday night he was certain it was where he belonged. It was the only place where he felt he could hide; and he could make his office secure.

Gregory drank two cups of Assam then started to distribute his belongings about his room. He was relieved to see there was enough space in the filing cabinets and cupboards to stow everything away. For his love of a tidy office was now compounded by his love of a tidy home.

He went for a walk, had a meal in an empty restaurant, returned to the branch and sat in his manager's chair. He did the main crossword in The Sunday Telegraph, and the one in The Observer. After which he locked the door of the outer office, and barricaded it with desks. Then he locked the door of the inner office. He put on some long woollen underwear, a pair of pyjamas and a jumper. He slept almost at once and did not wake until the rush hour of the following morning.

The next few days were a period of experimentation for Gregory, and it took him almost three weeks to establish a new routine. The biggest breakthrough was discovering a dry cleaner's on Euston Road where the staff were busy and unfriendly. It was not the sort of place where he would have to give an account of himself.

However the cleaner's would only deal with his shirts and suits; they would not take his underwear and socks. These therefore he decided to wear twice and throw away, as he could afford to be extravagant with his smalls. And, fearing suspicion, he never asked the dry cleaner's about pyjamas. Thus he wore a pair for a week and replaced them; and decided he would go to Marks and Spencer's on the second and fourth Tuesday of every month. Gregory thought he could go to their shop in Oxford Street every fortnight or so without becoming a recognised face.

His food and household things he mostly bought at the Tesco's Metro Store on the other side of Covent Garden. These visits he supplemented with one trip a week to the supermarket in Drury Lane; in which he decided he would spend no more than £20, as the shop was within half a mile of the branch.

Gregory saw newspapers as his greatest danger. So for these he went to the W.H.Smith's at Charing Cross Station: it was not a place where an individual was likely to be noticed. However given that he normally bought two or three each day it was not practicable to only buy them there; but he resolved to visit no other newsagent's more frequently than once a fortnight, and tried to buy no more than one newspaper at a time.

After a break of many months he returned to the hairdresser's in Marchmont Street which he had been visiting for years. It contained three chairs for customers, and two Greek barbers, who never said anything to Gregory but, 'Hello', 'the usual', 'thank you', and 'good bye'.

He scrupulously shunned all the shops on Holborn which he had visited when he had a job. All the shop assistants knew the branch was closed, and would have been surprised at his return. Gregory did not wish to invent a new job for himself. He preferred to hide than lie.

Thus Gregory managed to shut himself off from the world in central London. In a peculiar moment of whimsy he thought of changing his name to Mr. Anonymity Manifest; but decided his own name would serve as well. He still asked himself the question he had asked in Bromley whilst packing his bags, 'Gregory, what are you doing?'

And still he didn't know the answer. 'What else can I do?' was all he could say in reply.

Gregory thought often about the house he had abandoned. Not that he wanted to return there. The idea of going back to Bromley was fearful: he would be too exposed to the living and the dead. Yet though he couldn't bear the thought of retreating to his family's home, he wanted it to be left in peace. It pained him to think somebody might break in and ransack the place.

However he feared the police as much as he feared burglars. A broken window or a door left open might have alerted his neighbours to his absence. But even without a robbery he feared he would be reported missing. Yet why the police would care he had no idea: he was entitled not to live in Bromley.

But doubt chafed his mind. He did feel hunted, and it was natural to assume that as he was hiding he was being sought. Though he didn't believe the police would scour London for him; and he didn't imagine they would search his old office, unless a clue directed them there. He thought the police would try and trace him via his bank account.

Thus he paid for every thing with cash and never used a service till within the Circle Line. He even occasionally went as far as Oxford and Eastbourne to withdraw money. It was as if he felt wanted by the police, but not very much.

But from himself there was no hiding. It did not please Gregory to consider how he had come to his present pass, but he couldn't avoid the question. He spent hours in his manager's chair surveying his past. More than any other period Gregory dwelt on the first fifteen years of his career: on his twenties and thirties in Fleet Street.

It was here he felt he had made the mistake which had led him to his present solitude. Though to find a moment when his life had gone wrong was beyond him. All his days seemed alike. He had been concerned about his job and his family. He had not really troubled himself about finding a wife. He had ignored romance until he had arrived at Holborn. But by then he was too settled at home to escape. He yearned now for Hilary. He had a vision of her living alone somewhere, facing an old age as barren as his. He thought now that when he left her he had acted out of weakness and not brotherly compassion.

Gregory felt he had been sentenced to live by himself as a punishment for having spurned love. But there had been no one day when he had made a decision to do this: he had shaped his life as a young man unknowingly through habit. He had deprived himself of this joy, and consequently of all joy. And the things he now wanted were so simple – a wife and two children: just a moderately pretty wife, moderately intelligent, and a few years younger than himself; and two children, not prize winners, just children who avoided borstal.

Gregory wanted to be in love. He thought it would be bliss to be allowed to hold someone. His only contact with other humans was when he touched a shop assistant's hand while paying for something. For Gregory this counted as a pleasure.

He was driven to despair by the thought that he wanted something that was common, natural and impossible. To be what he wanted he would have had to go back and talk to his younger self and explain the future. Gregory felt that if he could have done this he could have been happy.

But despite his misery he kept up appearances. He dressed as he had always dressed for the office: grey suit, white shirt, red tie, polished brogues. He continued in this style because he liked it, and because he wanted to hide the oddity of his life. He wanted no one who looked at him to think, 'Oh, there's a man who lives in an empty office.' He accepted that his fear was unreasonable, but it endured.

Gregory had too many lonely hours of freedom for his mind to regain its equilibrium. Once he had settled into his new routine he suffered as he had in Bromley from want of occupation. The emptiness was not quite as bad however, partly because his arrangements were improvised and thus consumed more time. Washing, for instance, involved heating water on his stoves; then he had to heat some more to shave. And as he was determined not to do any shopping locally he spent many hours walking about central London. Which not only helped to use up each day but was a pleasure in itself.

For the large tracts of time that were left over from his chores Gregory resorted to his perennial crosswords; and novels; and increasingly, the view from his windows. He found pleasure on sitting on a stool and watching the street through the blinds; and the idea occurred to Gregory that he was a natural spectator.

Though he remained as much a spectator of himself as he was of the world; and he easily slipped from considering the latter to the former. Even when trying to break his own speed record for solving the Quick crossword in The Times Gregory was apt to lose himself in reverie. Either some clue would evoke a memory directly, or a clue would remind him of another clue encountered years before: and he would wonder when, and his mind would slide off into his past. Gregory lacked the substantial connection with the world that could take him away from himself. All his tasks were self imposed; he needed duties to bind him to sanity.

Despite his corrosive introspection he slept better in Holborn than he had in Bromley: the ghosts of his office did not trouble him in the same way; and only occasionally did he fear that somebody would try and break in. However the nights were longer than he needed, for he was often awake at three o'clock. These early hours he decided to fill with cleaning.

With the exception of the outside of the windows his own room was always spotless, but he decided to tackle the rest of the branch; and gradually he returned it to a fitting state. The work was impeded though by his need to shift the furniture about by himself, which was not only laborious but distracting. For Gregory desks held memories. Who had sat where and when often preoccupied him on his rounds, and he could stand for an hour thinking over the shifting pattern of bank clerks.

Regardless of how much time he had spent reminiscing Gregory always stopped his cleaning before dawn. He would climb the stairs to the store room on the fourth floor, and stand by the window that gave him the best view along Holborn to the east. His favourite sunrises were those in the Rococo style, when a thin scattering of clouds would catch the light and turn the sky into a mix of pink, azure and orange. He did not know why he still liked the dawn, it seemed peculiar to gladly welcome the start of a hopeless day. Yet uncomprehending though he was, he infallibly stood at the window and watched.

On one winter's morning it occurred to Gregory that even if he was alone he still had the sky as his friend. However he came to question this as winter gave way to spring, and then to summer. He had never liked warm weather, it made him uncomfortable, and when physically ill-at-ease his shyness became self consciousness. He always felt too revealed in summer, and that summer was the hottest in years. Heat upon solitude undid Gregory.

After his routine had lasted five months he was forced to abandon it on Monday, 31st July, 1995, when he decided to go hungry rather than face the world. Gregory had become convinced that he did not look normal; for despite his best efforts in front of the mirror, he was sure his appearance revealed where he lived and why he was there.

More so than ever he regarded the branch as his sole refuge, and on the preceding weekend he had felt besieged. The temperature had been above ninety degrees, and late every night there had been crowds of people in the street. Gregory had constantly expected an assault upon the building.

On Sunday night he didn't sleep at all. He got up at his usual time, went upstairs and watched the sky slowly lighten. Gregory stood at the window for almost four hours, trying to summon the courage to go out and find some food while the streets were still empty. Yet he failed.

He thought about starving to death. It seemed an odd thing to do when there was ample to eat within half a mile and he had money. But he couldn't buy food without facing people. And not only was he hungry, he had no crosswords to do, and nothing to read. Gregory could see the nearest newsagent's, it was only across the road, but he might as well have been looking at France from Dover.

This self consciousness had not arisen in a day. He had been slowly racked by the idea that people were looking at him; and the more he had looked at other people to see if they were, the more he had caught their attention, and the more they had looked back.

This fear of inspection though was only his mind's superficial reaction to his predicament. His fundamental problem was that he thought he was worthless. He had once had value in his eyes, when he had a job and relatives to care for, but with nothing to do he thought he was nothing. Gregory didn't feel his existence justified itself. To regard himself as a valid human being he had to be somebody's tool. He wanted to be a social cog, not a discarded part.

Gregory had taken his self loathing, put it in the minds of others, and had seen it reflected in their faces. The people he most feared were those who seemed to be late for something. Before them he wanted to vanish. Indeed he thought it would be best to be a ghost; so that he could drift about London, watching, but not being seen by others, and thus remain free from their scorn.

Gregory thought the next best thing would be to go to a police station and confess. He would confess to living in trespass, but the branch was just a detail. He wanted to confess that he was an inadequate human being. He wanted to give up his pretences and publish his wretchedness before the eyes of the world. He wanted to be honest. But he thought that if everyone were to do that then the police stations would be mobbed; and besides, he hadn't the courage. So Gregory had carried on, visibly and unshriven.

Having decided he wouldn't eat Gregory went back to his manager's chair and fell into a troubled sleep. He dreamed of being with his family and of being ignored: he tried to shout at them but he was so fearful he could only manage a strangled moan. It was this sound though which woke him up. When he recovered he saw that it was five past one in the afternoon; and he was noticeably hungrier than before. The rest of the day and the following night continued this pattern of nightmare and hunger. It only stopped at five a.m. when Gregory woke up sweating with frustration and fear.

Never in his life had Gregory gone without food. He didn't like the sensation in his body after thirty-six hours without eating, and he panicked. He thought that if he didn't do something immediately he would become too weak to save himself. His fleshed triumphed over his spirit and he washed and dressed.

With eyes fixed on the pavement Gregory hurried to Euston Station, and had breakfast in the remotest corner of the emptiest café. Then still with eyes cast down, he made his way to the supermarket in Drury Lane, and came away with three days' worth of provisions.

On regaining the branch he felt he had achieved something heroic, and sat with a cup of tea and a sense of triumph.

However he did not attempt to re-establish his routine as he knew his nerves could not cope. He could only respond to emergencies. He would dash to a newsagent's when he had the courage and buy every newspaper with a crossword worth solving; and beyond that he only went out when he needed food, candles or gas canisters.

He felt he couldn't go to the dry cleaner's any more, nor to Marks and Spencer's, and so took to washing his clothes by hand. He cut the leads off two telephones, and strung them between the metal racks in the store room, which then became his drying room.

Sadly he lacked an iron, and did not feel equal to shopping for one. However his shirts dried without many creases, and Gregory thought they would be acceptable under a jacket. For in order to look normal Gregory still went out in a suit, in weather which saw most other men in cotton trousers and short sleeved shirts. And once he stopped ironing Gregory no longer walked around with his jacket undone.

He therefore restricted himself to shopping before ten o'clock in the morning. He found that if the streets were cool and deserted then he felt comfortable; which was a relief, as he feared that his paranoia was developing into agoraphobia. He also found that if the pavements were crowded, so that no one could more than glance at him, then he did not suffer badly – once he had submerged himself in the throng.

However if people had time enough to study him for a few seconds, then he felt as if were going about without his skin on. Even if the person coming towards him looked gentle and relaxed, Gregory's face would be forced down as if some weight were resting on his head. He would squirm, his legs would tremble, and he would ask himself over and over why people thought he looked so odd.

Sometimes Gregory's agitation would force him to turn into a side street, or to cross the road. Alternatively, he would pretend his shoe lace had come undone and would crouch down until his panic had passed. Whatever his stratagem though, he felt wretched.

Gregory spent hours in front of the mirror trying to ascertain the manner of his oddness. Some days he would assure himself that he wasn't odd, and that the problem was only in his mind; yet it still required much courage for him to walk about in public.

On the days on which his courage failed he went hungry; and Gregory lived in expectation of his nerve failing completely, and of his consequent death by starvation. The visit was thus in part a relief.

They arrived on a Thursday morning, just after Gregory had walked down the stairs to go out. He was about to unlock the iron grill when he heard the front door open. He had placed three pieces of wood and an empty tin against the main door; and when Gregory heard the tin bounce, roll and come to a stop, he thought in all certainty, 'It's over.'

Yet he did not surrender himself. He walked on his toes to the door of the stairwell which opened onto the ground floor. He stopped long enough to hear one man say, 'This all should have been cleared a long time ago,' and another answer, 'Doesn't matter, it'll only take a week.' Then quietly he fled to his office.

He locked himself in and pushed two desks against the door. He sat on one of these, and put the key back in the lock to prevent somebody else doing so from the other side. Then he thought, 'Why, Gregory, it's over, why?' But he didn't want to be hurried out of his home, he wanted first to think.

Gregory spent twenty minutes sitting on the desk before the visitors reached the second floor. He gripped the key and felt another being pushed against it.

'There's something in the way,' one man said.

'Isn't it vacant?' the other asked.

One man hit the door mightily, and shouted, 'Hello!' Two feet away Gregory flinched, but held onto his key in silence. Three more times he flinched as the door was beaten. Then one man led the other away, whilst expressing his puzzlement and promising that the branch would be cleared after the weekend.

An hour later the visitors left and Gregory let go of the key. He lay down on the desk and remained prostrate until the afternoon.

When he got up it was with the spirit of a man who had been tried, judged and sentenced. Gregory now knew the worst, and the worst seemed better than carrying on. Against the alternative his sentence could be seen as a rescue, and he walked about his office and saw it with new eyes. Again it meant to him what it had on the day of his return from Bromley. Now though he was facing the last good-bye. A second return would not be possible. Unless, as he feared, the preparations for his farewell were interrupted.

Warily he moved the desks and unlocked the door. Though he told himself he was being mad, he suspected that one of the visitors had silently returned and was waiting for him below. He had to see. After pausing on the landing Gregory went down the steps with extraordinary care one at a time. When he reached the ground floor he stopped and listened for ten minutes, and then peeped through the keyhole. He turned the handle and pushed, and the door opened to reveal no one. He cautiously looked about. Once he was satisfied that he was alone he reassembled his crude alarm against the entrance from the street. Then, locking the stairwell door behind him, Gregory went and made his office ready for the next visit.

Within an hour he was done. Though he thought his arrangements could have been improved by a visit to a hardware store. He was however reluctant to go in case the visitors returned while he was out. One of them had clearly said that the building would be cleared after the weekend, but even so Gregory did not want to take the risk. He would wait until Friday lunchtime. He assumed that the branch would be emptied by the bank's property department, and, to judge by their reputation and his experience, once they had scattered into the pubs of Clerkenwell at twelve o'clock on a Friday they were unlikely to move again until the evening. If Gregory could wait until Friday lunchtime he would be safe until Monday.

He ate the last of his food and settled into his manager's chair. He dozed, unintentionally, and woke with a shock. He thought he had heard the empty tin bounce about downstairs. For twenty minutes he listened at his barricaded door, but the branch was quiet. As it was past five p.m. Gregory decided he must either have dreamt the noise, or heard something in the street. Feeling mortally tired Gregory went back to his chair, got undressed and climbed into his sleeping bag. He had often of late felt exhausted and yet failed to sleep for more than a couple of hours at a time; therefore he was surprised when he woke up at seven the next morning.

For a while he lay still, marvelling at how refreshed he felt. His torpor was gone, and the thought even occurred to him that it would be nice to go out. He extricated himself from his bag, and overflowing with gratitude paced up and down in his pyjamas. A burden had been lifted from him. Now he was a condemned man the world was a more cheerful place.

His only immediate fear was that there would be a second visit that morning; but given his sense of well being he doubted it could happen. 'I'm going to have my last weekend,' he told himself.

Despite this confidence he quickly washed and dressed to be ready for a visitor by eight o'clock. But none came. By ten o'clock he was impatient. Having been afflicted by self consciousness for weeks he wanted to go out and test himself. He thought the desire was strange as very soon it wouldn't matter; but he did dearly want his mind to be healed before the end.

At half-past-ten he gave in to his impatience, and went down the stairs and out into the alley. Without thinking where he was going he set off towards Covent Garden. He was disappointed by his reaction to people, because he had hoped for a complete recovery and found himself merely much better.

Before he had gone five yards a middle aged woman of unremarkable appearance turned the corner and walked towards him. Gregory had to look down, but he did so with a calm expression and not one of fear. And he found that this was his reaction to everyone he met. Gregory decided he had ascended from paranoia to shyness; and to test himself further headed towards Café Valerie.

To his relief he was greeted by the waitress he knew best, a stout, blonde, Italian woman, who seemed to live in a state of perpetual joy. Her smile and welcome gave him the courage to speak; and for the first time in two months he had a conversation. His half of it was full of lies, but they were confident lies.

Despite this triumph once Gregory had eaten he became fearful. He paid, and went back up Drury Lane and along Holborn, indifferent in his hurry to the gaze of others. The last two hundred yards he ran.

He examined the front door and peered through the windows, then he ran round to the back. Everything was as it was. He opened the door, then the iron grill as quietly as he could, and with great caution searched the building. Then he called himself some names.

After Gregory had recovered he decided he should have his hair cut, and after that go shopping: he wanted to buy a hammer and a packet of nails, a new suit, a new pair of shoes, three shirts and two ties.

He went to his barber's in Marchmont Street, and found one of the Greeks sitting alone with his cutting chairs all empty. The man did not remark on Gregory's long absence nor his long hair. He wielded his scissors and razor with his normal grave manner; and only departed from his wonted routine to the extent of giving Gregory a quizzical look when he received a tip three times larger than usual. In exchange though he offered only a singular, 'Thanks.'

Gregory went to Marks and Spencer's. He wasn't confident while finding his suit. Words tripped out of him and fell awkwardly, and he had to start several times to ask for a 40 Regular, plain, dark grey, three piece suit, before he was shown what he wanted. As always though there was a suit in his size in stock ready for him to take away.

While he walked back along Oxford Street he regretted his lingering nerves, but in deference to his achievement he acknowledged that two days previously it would have been impossible for him even to have entered a department store. Then to raise his spirits he turned right into New Bond Street and headed for the Burlington Arcade. This Regency relic of boutiques had long attracted Gregory, but only as a window gazer. Now he aimed to buy.

As he approached the arcade he told himself not to rush, but to cool down first, stop sweating, and then make his purchase. So with deliberate slowness he moved from shoe shop to shoe shop, until he was moderately calm and had decided which pair of black brogues he wanted to buy. Then he went in. The door spring creaked, a bell rung, and a shop assistant stood up and smiled. Gregory said, 'I would like a pair of those please, size nine and a half.' And in five minutes he was out and away.

Gregory hurried to the churchyard of St. James's, Piccadilly, and sat down on an empty bench. He decided he had to take off his jacket: did so, closed his eyes, and slowly relaxed once more.

He did not however let go of the plastic bag which contained his new brogues. He had been tempted to tell the shop assistant that he would wear these, and that his old ones could be thrown away. Gregory though had never been equal to grand gestures and was certainly not so now.

He opened his eyes and checked to see if anyone was looking at him. They weren't. He pulled the box out of the bag. He removed the lid, unwrapped the tissue, and admired his shoes. Gregory looked about him again and changed brogues.

They had cost him £200; which, he reflected, might seem a lot for shoes, but £200 wasn't a vast amount, he could easily afford it, and owning them gave him considerable joy. Given his other habits he could always have bought his shoes in the Burlington Arcade. But he hadn't. He had gone to a shop off Bromley High Street and made his choice from whatever he had found there; and, he realised with self contempt, he had even seen his narrowness as a virtue. Gregory studied his brogues and regretted that only at the end was he prepared to treat himself to a harmless luxury; before he would have regarded them as insufficiently suburban.

He put his old shoes in the bag, put on his jacket, and picked up the carrier containing his

Marks and Spencer's suit. He walked out of the churchyard and threw his old brogues into the first bin he passed. Then he walked down an alley into Jermyn Street, and at Herbie Frogg's bought three expensive white shirts, and two costly ties: one red with white polka dots, and the other plain black. He hailed a taxi and said, 'Holborn', loudly. Once he had got in the driver made a comment about the weather and Gregory had his second conversation of the day.

As he approached Holborn Gregory became anxious again, lest the branch had been visited in his absence. He searched it once more but found no sign of any intrusion. He made himself a cup of tea, marvelled at what he had accomplished that day, and thought about how little time he had left. Then he went shopping again and returned with food and an iron.

Gregory slept well on Friday night but awoke with the thought that it was his last weekend. He asked himself if there was an alternative and answered by declaring it to be a stupid question. Worried by his fear though he climbed out of his sleeping bag and got ready. He put on one of his new white shirts, a pair of beige cotton trousers, a navy blue blazer, and his new shoes.

Then he stood and faced the noose he had prepared. It dangled down from the waterpipe that crossed the ceiling en route to the toilets. His hanging rope was actually an old cable that had lain in the store room for years. It was thick, long and black: the sole remaining part of a machine which not even Gregory could remember. The cable had been the source of a running joke in the branch. Every once in a while somebody had said, 'Shall we throw it away?' And the answer had always been, 'No, it will come in useful one day.' And it had.

Gregory started to laugh, and his laughter grew louder, until it could have been heard from the ground to the fourth floor, if there had been anyone to hear it. Then he cried, but more softly. He sat on his manager's chair and stayed there until his tears stopped. Then he washed his face, took a red silk handkerchief from one of the cupboards, folded it, put it in his breast pocket, and went out.

He went to Café Valerie for breakfast, and the waitress told him he looked nice; and Gregory was deeply grateful. After he had eaten he went to a newsagent's in Drury Lane, bought every serious newspaper, and passed the day in an orgy of crosswords.

By early evening he was sated and could stomach no more clues. He closed his Chamber's, Twentieth Century Dictionary, his Pear's, Cyclopaedia, and his Brewer's, Phrase and Fable. He made a neat pile of his papers and sat and looked about him.

Gregory wondered what his colleagues would have thought if they could have seen him. He hoped they would have liked his new shoes, and wouldn't have mocked him for his extravagance. And as for his manner of living he didn't know what they would have said. He studied his room more carefully. It seemed odd that the same place could have been an office, a home, a gaol, and a gallows. Gregory laughed, and once more his laughter travelled up and down the stairwell.

He went out and returned with fish and chips and a bottle of Burgundy; and with the help of the wine slept better than he feared.

On Sunday he awoke with the thought that it was his last whole day. He didn't dwell on this but got ready quickly. He wore his new suit, with his new red tie; but again he went to Café Valerie for breakfast.

As the Italian waitress had worked on Saturday he assumed she wouldn't be there on Sunday; but she was. And she said, 'You're still looking nice.'

Gregory sat in the corner on the left with The Observer, and wished that things could have been different. He continued to think this as he ate his smoked salmon and drank his cappuccino.

A German couple arrived with their teenage daughter and took the table beside Gregory's. He liked them. They spoke to the waitress in English; and he wanted to speak to them. He wanted to say, 'Hello, I'm a human being too.' But he couldn't. Instead he raised his newspaper to hide his tears.

Slowly Gregory regained his composure and lowered The Observer. The Germans left and he completed a crossword; then he nodded at the waitress and she brought him his bill. It came to £8-75 and he put a £20 note on the saucer. He wanted to say good-bye to the waitress and thank her for the happiness she had brought him. But the words wouldn't come and so he kissed her.

Gregory Gun kissed the plump Italian waitress and fled. He left the café with a crimson face, but by the time he had crossed the piazza his pallor had returned and his heart was filled with joy. With the taste of the waitress on his lips he walked across London towards Regent's Park.

The weather was cooler than it had been, yet still Gregory was glad he had left his waistcoat at home. He went up Charing Cross Road, then Tottenham Court Road, before turning left and stopping in front of the Post Office Tower. He remembered he had been excited by it once. He had been twenty-five when it was finished, and as soon as he was able to book seats he had taken April to the revolving restaurant at the top. April hadn't liked going round in the air and they hadn't stayed for dessert; but he had loved the experience, and the views were still vivid in his mind. It seemed to Gregory that for just one hour he had been part of the Sixties.

He walked on. He wondered if the plump Italian waitress would like to work in a revolving restaurant. Then thoughts of the next day crowded into his mind and he forgot about her.

He walked on through empty streets until he emerged at the top of Portland Place, where he was brought to a stop by the traffic on the Marylebone Road. When the lights changed he crossed over into the park; but did so with some concern as he wasn't sure of the extent of his recovery. That summer he had found parks to be particularly fearful places, given the propensity of people to sit about in them and watch. Gregory had come to hate people sitting on benches. They were even worse than people who walked towards him. At least with the latter he could find a pretext to stand still; but when people were on a bench he had to go on, however wretched and contorted his face, and however much his legs shook.

Gregory decided he would be safer in a crowd than by himself, and so turned left and followed the edge of the boating lake. Although he had to look down several times on catching someone's eye, he didn't feel the people about him saw him as a monstrosity. He didn't feel calm, but he didn't feel threatened. He was a commonplace, middle-aged man, taking a stroll in a park on a Sunday morning. Gregory kept telling himself this.

Encouraged by his modest degree of security he decided to strike out. When he reached the corner of the lake opposite the mosque Gregory abandoned the shore and headed off into the open park.

Gregory walked briskly for five minutes then stopped in the shade of a lone tree. There was a group of Americans close by playing with a Frisbee, and he studied them with interest. They were all in their twenties and thirties, and though they were dressed in shorts and t-shirts Gregory assumed they worked in the same office. He liked the way they shouted at each other and chased the orange disk; for even though he wasn't very good at living himself, he liked watching other people doing it.

However his pleasure was abruptly halted by the site of two policemen walking towards him. They seemed relaxed as they sauntered closer in their short sleeved shirts, but Gregory looked at his watch, made a mock gesture of surprise, and went back the way he came.

Gregory didn't know if they had noticed it was him. He imagined that the wanted-posters in police stations would now be curled and faded; but he was certain he would be arrested if the policemen looked at his face.

Gregory walked as fast as he could whilst trying to behave naturally. On coming to a junction of footpaths he turned left, then stopped two hundred yards later, knelt down and pretended to tie up a shoe lace. Gregory glanced over his shoulder and saw the policemen turn left, and head once more towards him.

He hurried on. They were younger men and despite his lead he was certain he would be caught if he ran; so he carried on walking, right across the park.

After what seemed like several miles he came to a tea shop. There were a dozen or so tables outside, and one of them was free. To his right he could see a couple heading towards it, but Gregory got there first, and cared nothing for the shocked look on their faces.

He moved his chair so that his back faced the path and waited for the policemen to go by, or arrest him. He looked at his watch, and stared at the second-hand as it made its slow progress. He told himself his fate would be settled within three minutes.

'What would you like, please?' the waitress asked, and Gregory jumped.

'Sorry,' she said with evident concern.

'Tea, sorry, tea.'

'Darjeeling, Earl Grey, Orange Pekoe, English Breakfast or Assam?'

'Assam, Assam.'

'A pot or a cup?'

'Cup, a cup, please.'

'Thank you.'

The young girl walked away and Gregory turned round. One of the policemen was talking into his radio. Gregory turned back and stared very hard at the table. The waitress brought his cup of Assam tea, and he stared very hard at that.

He did want to drink it, but his hands were shaking too much, and so he sat on them. 'Gregory, behave normally,' he implored.

The policemen walked past. Gregory closed his eyes and tried to count to one hundred; but he only reached sixty-seven before he opened them again. Gregory glanced to his right then stared once more at his cup. The policemen had stopped within a hundred yards of him, and they were both talking into their radios.

For five minutes Gregory sat rigid over his Assam tea; but the policemen went no further away. He didn't dare shift his eyes, but he could hear them.

'Is there something wrong with it?' the waitress asked.

'Yes, it's fine, I'm not feeling very well.'

Gregory stood up in panic, and having done that started to hurry away. Then he realised he hadn't paid, and hurried back, terrified that the girl would call the police. He put his hand in his side-pocket, pulled out several pounds worth of change, put all of the coins onto the table, and saw two of them roll off onto the ground. Then he ran.

He ran across the park. People looked at him, but his horror of this was far less than his horror of being arrested.

Gregory ran until the sweat poured off him and his heart threatened to hammer its way through his chest. When he could go no further he collapsed by a sapling, and lay in its paltry shade, about thirty yards from the boundary fence of the zoo. He thought he would never see the branch again.

When he had recovered slightly he looked about him and discovered he was alone. The Metropolitan Police Force was not closing in, and there was no lynch mob. He climbed to his feet and looked in every direction, but still he could see no pursuers; and only a distant elephant seemed interested in him. Despite this he pressed on, albeit more slowly.

Gregory took off his jacket and followed the fence until he came to a gate out of the park. He crossed a road, walked over a bridge above a canal, crossed another road, and wandered onto Primrose Hill. He didn't know where he was going but his instinct drove him away from where he had last seen the police. He meandered across the grass and stumbled up the slope to the top. There was an empty place on the end of a bench and Gregory sat down, and almost fell off.

'Tomorrow I shall be dead,' he thought with relief and fear. Then he thought it would be good to die straight away; but he wanted to die in the branch.

Gregory sat on Primrose Hill for two hours. The people on the bench beside him left, and others took their place, several times over; but Gregory remained, gazing across London. In the distance was Sydenham Hill with its two radio masts. On the far slope of the hill was Penge, then came Beckenham, then Bromley. Twice every working day for thirty-four years he had gone through Sydenham Hill in the train tunnel, but he would go through it no more. Gregory would never see Bromley again. He was glad.

Slowly he recovered. His last walk was proving more eventful than he would have liked; but he hoped, having escaped the horrors of the park, that he would at least be able to get home safely.

He was on the point of leaving when a new crowd of people arrived: six adults and three boys. One of the men wore a skull cap, and Gregory assumed they were Jews from Golders Green on a family trip to London. One of the women took great pains to interest her son in the view, but he was staunchly unimpressed. He told her he was thirsty. He told her this several times with increasing volume; then he slowly shouted, 'I-want-a-drink!' In a tone which implied that the only possible reason he had not been pandered to, was that he had not been heard clearly.

To Gregory's surprise the man in the skull cap pulled a bright green yo-yo out of the sleeve of his shoulder bag, and said, 'David, can you do this?' Gregory had expected the child to be hit very hard. Instead the man flicked his wrist and the yo-yo went down and up. Twice more the child complained he was thirsty, and each time the man flicked his wrist. Then he shot the yo-yo forward, off the top of the hill and brought it back; and the boy implored to be allowed to play with it. Gently the man explained the trick, and all three boys crowded round.

Gregory thought of his family, and how he had been treated. He thought he had given far more than he had received, and that his end was the consequence of his enforced generosity.

For a while he was bitter, and hated himself for his weakness, and his family for its tyranny.

Eventually though he shrugged his shoulders, 'But I am as I am.'

He stood up, put on his jacket, and walked away.

Gregory did not return to the branch via Regent's Park. Instead he walked along the main road which skirted it to Baker Street, then escaped from the traffic and made his way through the side streets to Holborn. The walk took Gregory an hour and though he badly wanted a drink he pressed on, as he didn't want to take the risk of stopping in a café.

Instead he bought a loaf, a pint of milk and The Sunday Telegraph, in a newsagent's. And when he paid and said, 'Thank you,' he realised it was the last occasion on which he would speak to somebody. He stopped at the door, half turned, again said, 'Thank you,' then added, 'Good bye;' and got a, 'Bye,' and a nod in response.

Gregory returned to the branch and locked himself in with relief and sorrow. 'Hello bank; good bye world,' he thought; then checked the building for any sign of intrusion. He found none.

Gregory made himself a pot of tea, and a pile of buttered toast; then sat at his desk to complete his last two crosswords. He took his time, and felt a growing sense of regret at each solved clue; but dawdle though he did he finished them eventually, and then was just left with himself.

He tried to escape from his thoughts by cleaning his office. Then he browsed his shelf of novels, but he didn't have time to re-read even the shortest. He thought about reading the newspaper, but news had long since lost its interest for him. So he washed and shaved, and set the alarm. He tried to sleep the night away, but he couldn't.

Gregory got up and polished his brogues. He regretted having run across the park in them, but he could safely say it wouldn't happen again. He put on his third new shirt, his new black tie, and once more his suit. For the first time he put on his waistcoat. As a rule he didn't wear one between Whitsun and Michaelmas, but he was prepared to make an exception for his last day. He put the kitchen table below the noose, and by half-past-midnight he was ready.

Gregory sat on his manager's chair and succumbed to introspection. He set off on the familiar journey through his past and again tried to find the point of failure: the moment when he had taken the track to his current plight.

But as he thought again about the incidents and phases of his life he shook his head repeatedly; for he suspected at last that he never had any choice of route, his life just happened to be a dull plod through an arid valley.

'I am as I am,' he said out loud to his candle lit office in the quiet of a Sunday night. Over and over he had searched in his mind for some track that would have led him out of his dismal valley onto the hills above. Yet the sides had always been too steep, and the promising tracks to the left and right had always been detours that wound back to the main path. Not that he had explored them, but he knew it was so.

Gregory thought it would have been nice to have lived, but that it wasn't his fate. He was born to be Gregory Gun, to suffer and serve things which would die before him, and then to die alone. His family and the branch had vanished, his mistake had been to try and struggle on.

'But why should anything have been different?' he asked himself, 'Nobody promised love and happiness.' He accepted the truth of this and he cried.

Gregory cried until dawn, then he watched the sky brighten through the grime of his windows. At six o'clock his alarm went off, and he barricaded the outer door, and nailed the top half of it to its frame.

He looked out of his windows once more and waited for the builders to arrive.

He stood waiting for an hour, anxiously peering left and right, and glancing at the clock; yet no builders came. Indeed he saw few people of any type. He thought that many people were probably away from their offices on holiday; but as the clock moved past seven-thirty he became increasingly perplexed. Then he ran across the room and started pulling his belongings out from one of the cupboards.

After he had cleared two shelves he found his long unused diary. He thumbed through it frantically until he reached August, only to realise he didn't know what the date was. He grabbed hold of The Sunday Telegraph, looked at the top of the page, looked in diary, and discovered it was Bank Holiday Monday.

Gregory rushed back to the window. There was still no sign of any builders. With very different feelings he looked at the clock, and watched it creep towards eight; and when the minute hand stood upright he punched the air and shouted, 'Yes!' Gregory had another day to live and he collapsed into his manager's chair feeling suddenly exhausted.

'But what if they're just late?' he thought, 'Maybe at ten they'll be here.' Yet he didn't believe it. He told himself that if they were going to work on a Bank Holiday they would start and finish early. Gregory was sure of this. Though he waited until nine before he got changed; which also allowed him some time to revive.

He put on a short sleeved shirt, and a pair of cotton trousers, and he was tempted by his sandals, but still could not resist his brogues. He put his keys in one pocket of his trousers, and a £20 note and a handkerchief in the other; and then realised he couldn't go out until he had dismantled the barricade by the door, and pulled the nails out of the frame.

The desks he moved in ten minutes, but it took him more than half-an-hour to extract the nails; and if he had not by chance bought a hammer with a claw he probably would have been trapped.

Finally, after he heaved out the twelfth nail, Gregory ran down the stairs. 'I never expected to do this again,' he thought, and repeated his thought at each landing and each door. In the alley behind the bank he briefly danced a jig.

He crossed Holborn, but stopped half-way, and looked up and down, and scratched his head and smiled. 'No builders,' he thought. He crossed to the other pavement and looked at the branch. 'Unviolated,' he thought. He walked round the corner into Kingsway and looked at the pavement in the shade, and the pavement in the sun. 'Shade,' he thought.

At first Gregory walked in the shade, but then he crossed to the right and walked in the sun; and then he walked in the middle of the road.

A group of tourists emerged from a side street and stood on the sunny pavement. Gregory headed for them and said, 'Good morning.' And they, in American accents, said, 'Good morning,' back: and Gregory felt no fear at all. He looked at the sky and once more it seemed like his friend.

At the end of Kingsway Gregory stopped between the giant columns of Bush House, and admired the solidity of the brass doors which lay behind them; and it suddenly occurred to Gregory what a good thing the B.B.C. was. He thought about his childhood and the radio. Then he thought he would like to be reprieved for a day every day: then he could live.

Gregory set off down Fleet Street. It was almost deserted and he was able to stop and look at the buildings undisturbed, and think about the changes that had taken place during the twenty years since he had worked there. It seemed ludicrous and sad that the Telegraph and Express buildings had been abandoned by their newspapers. When he had worked in Fleet Street it had been an exciting place; not that he had been part of the excitement, but he had been near it, and he had got his crosswords warm. Now Fleet Street was the same as any street.

His first branch was still there though. There had been rumours that it would close along with the one in Holborn. Then it was rumoured that it would be in the next wave of closures. But it was still there, and he peered through the glass and wished he could go in.

Gregory walked away. He turned off Fleet Street and went along the short alley that led to St. Bride's. It too was shut and Gregory sat alone in the churchyard.

He had sung in St. Bride's. The manager, the chief cashier, and several clerks from the Fleet Street Branch had been amongst the amateurs in the choir. Gregory had been a subdued bass. He had been too aware of his deficiencies to sing freely; but he had contributed and enjoyed himself. Yet after a few years the manager retired, his replacement had no interest in St. Bride's or singing; and the other choristers lost their enthusiasm. Gregory regretted this now.

He looked at the far church door; imagined himself as he would have been thirty years before, leaving with his colleagues after two hours' practice of an evening; and walked away.

He walked along the lane that curved its way down towards Blackfriars Bridge, with the intention of crossing the Thames; but he stopped on seeing the once familiar art nouveau façade of the Black Friar pub. It was where he used to drink a couple of pints after singing hymns. He crossed the road and looked up at the statue of the laughing Dominican. Gregory remembered drinking his health on a summer evening with his manager. And he remembered thinking that one day he would be a manager and buy his clerks drinks; and life had seemed predictable and secure.

As it was he was unable to buy even himself a pint, for at that hour the pub was shut.

He turned away to his right, and saw Blackfriars Station, and he realised he could go somewhere for the day, if he so wished. The idea took Gregory by surprise, and he smiled and shook his head, but then he asked himself, 'But why not?'

Gregory went into the station and up the escalator to the platforms and ticket office. He stood looking at the departure boards and thinking, 'Why not, Gregory, why not?'

Then to his right he noticed a slice of the old Blackfriars Station which had been saved. It was a section of wall which contained a list of destinations. On studying it he found it ran in roughly alphabetical order from Antwerp to Wiesbaden. Beckenham was there, beside Baden-Baden; and Crystal Palace was there too, beside Calais.

The French name struck him quiet hard. 'Why not go to France, Gregory? Why not live?'

The names of Lyons, Paris and Cannes were in front of him, and also others which suddenly appealed.

His passport was in the branch. He could be back there in twenty minutes, and pack his bags and be in France that afternoon. Then he thought of what he could do in France, and he became excited by the idea; and he thought some more, and the dream began to fade.

He thought that for two or three weeks he might enjoy himself; but then he would have to move on, and move on again, then again, to escape his emptiness. But he couldn't move on forever.

He would get tired and settle in some hotel and quickly his life would become as strange and isolated as it was in Holborn. He imagined as a foreigner in France it would be even worse: he thought it would not be long before the children started throwing stones at him; then he would be arrested.

Everything was bound to be the same as it was in Holborn, wherever he went: be it Bromley, Normandy, or Bali. Wherever he went he would take himself with him.

For some time more he stood looking at the names thinking what he might do if he were somebody else; but eventually, with a shrug, he walked out of the station.

He left without thinking where he was going, and as he walked along realised he was somewhere new; for he had never ventured past the Black Friar in that direction. The road seemed like a huge concrete and stone trench, and it was rank with the dirt of a long, hot summer.

He walked for five minutes in misery. Then on his right he found a small Seventeenth Century church called St. Benet's. He was as surprised as if he had discovered it on the hard shoulder of a motorway. It appeared that somebody had forgotten to destroy the building, so alien did it look amongst its surroundings.

Gregory would have liked to have sat in St. Benet's to think and rest, but it seemed so obviously shut he didn't try the door. Instead he turned about and saw ahead of him a lane leading up St. Paul's; and so crossed the road, climbed the hill, and went round St. Paul's until he found an empty seat in the cathedral yard.

Yet though the yard was more akin to a garden than a cemetery he couldn't relax due to the number of people milling about. He shut his eyes and tried to forget those around him, but he couldn't free his mind. It occurred to Gregory that he could go inside St. Paul's, but he thought it would be equally disturbing. He knew that if he wanted somewhere quiet to think he could simply go back to Holborn; but for months he had been doing all his thinking in the branch.

Gregory wondered if his thoughts would be different now if he had done his thinking somewhere else. Then he told himself that thoughts weren't dependent upon location, then he told himself that they were. Yet, he considered, if they were then a man might reach different conclusions in a large, bright room, than he would in a small, dark room: which would make truth the poodle of the weather and the builders. Gregory decided that thoughts in general might be dependent on location; but his weren't. His depended upon him being a banker or an ex-banker.

Gregory got up and walked on. He headed further into the City and crossed the road and went along Cheapside. He passed a branch of Lloyd's, then one of National Westminster, then one of the Royal Bank of Scotland. They evidently were all still wanted, unlike Gregory's branch.

His mind was distracted from this sour thought by the eccentric spire of St. Mary-le-bow: gloriously evident in the morning sun. He followed it with his eye up from the street far into the air, and he wondered how many times in his life he had seen it without looking at it.

He stopped at the entrance of the church and studied the solid wooden doors, and the row of solid iron spikes which emerged from them. And above the spikes he found a row of cherubs, each with a laughing face framed in its wings. Gregory wasn't sure if they were mocking him for being shut out in the street, or if they were urging him to hurry up and be dead.

He gazed at them, trying to understand, until his neck ached. Then he moved away, and, as if to spite him, he found that a branch of the Yorkshire Bank had been built into a corner of the church.

Gregory turned about, crossed Cheapside, and headed back to Holborn. He could accept that life was impossible for him without a job, and that he had lost the only job he could do; but he found it hard to stomach his branch having been put on the unwanted list when so many more had escaped.

If his branch had survived he knew he would still be the old Gregory Gun. He could have lived if he could have worked. As it was he was too old to be useful, and too young to be idle. But he thought he could be useful – in a bank. Men used to work until they were sixty-five or seventy, he told himself: if he could have carried on until he was old he could have retired to a home, and pottered about in a garden with a sun hat and a couple of newspapers.

Dreams of what might have been occupied him during the half hour he took to amble to Holborn Circus; and there he stood, with no people and no traffic in sight, and looked at the branch of National Westminster, and thought, 'If only.'

If he had been wise enough to join another bank or another branch he wouldn't be going back for the last time.

But then, after a few minutes, he thought that all such men as he might be doomed; and he felt a little better. He thought that perhaps, within a decade, all the branches might be closed; and that throughout England middle-managers would be sitting at home stupefied by idleness and boredom. It was a comforting thought because it meant he wouldn't have suffered alone: he was more of a forerunner than an oddity. Also it meant that his choice of branch wasn't that significant – he couldn't imagine he would ever have been one of the managers to have lasted to the end. And if he hadn't made a bad choice there was less to regret: there was no error to reproach himself with.

A belief in his own competence was one of the few remaining props to his self respect, and

Gregory was heartened by this line of reflection. With a quicker pace he walked on. He sought out an open newsagents; and again returned home for the last time with a pint of milk, a loaf of bread and a newspaper.

He made toast and tea; and he sat musing for a long time over what banks would be like without branches. 'All trunk,' he thought, and chuckled; 'or perhaps more like a Scots pine than an English oak.' And he chuckled again, even though he thought oaks to be superior by far.

Gregory picked up The Times, and sat down at his desk. He was glad that his last crossword would be in a daily newspaper and not a Sunday one; as he had never been able to give sufficient attention to Sunday crosswords to make them part of his routine: at least not while April was alive.

He considered making an attempt at his speed record, but he was too tired to make it worthwhile; and he preferred to savour his last crosswords rather than rush them. Yet he found the clues to the Quick that day to be too uninspired to be interesting; however, he greatly enjoyed the humour of the Cryptic.

He smiled when he wrote down, 'PLOUGHMANSLUNCH,' in response to, 10 ACROSS, 'Pub snack taken to till? (10,5).' He laughed when he filled in the squares with, 'LOHENGRIN,' for, 2 DOWN, 'Wagner's work is long, involved with Rhine (9).' And when he answered, 23 DOWN, 'In movie, sailed out of sight? (4,4,3,4),' with, 'GONEWITHTHEWIND,' he was so amused by the appositeness of the last clue of the last crossword, that he beat his head upon his desk.

When Gregory regained control of himself he rested his head upon his arms, closed his eyes, and, unintentionally, fell asleep.

He awoke in panic. It was twilight and he thought the builders were about to seize him. He stumbled from his desk to window, but he couldn't see any builders in the street. Fearing they were already in the branch he ran to the door of the outer office, and listened. He opened it slowly, cautiously made his way down the stairs, and returned relieved. He realised it was evening.

Gregory went back to the window and watched the street for a couple of minutes, then he went to the toilet. When he had finished he looked in the mirror and had a second shock: his face was disfigured. It was covered in grey blotches and blue streaks, and he stared at himself in fright. He tried to think of an illness that would so afflict his face, but he couldn't; and it occurred to him that it was the result of the anguish he had endured.

Yet after studying himself awhile he sighed in resignation, 'It doesn't matter now, Gregory, though, does it? No one is ever going to see you again, are they? No.' He agreed with himself, but he felt the need to cover the mirror.

He wandered about looking for something suitable, then his eyes fell on his newspaper, and he dashed back to the kitchen and started to wash. He had been sleeping on his crossword.

Once he had returned his face to its normal colour, he undressed and washed the rest of his body. Then he found some cologne and dabbed himself, then once more he put on his shirt and tie, and suit and brogues.

He was ready before midnight, and for a time stood in his office reflecting on how he should spend his last hours. He realised there were many parts of the branch which he hadn't visited for days;

indeed he thought he had been taking it for granted of late; so he decided on a final inspection.

Taking his torch he made his way down to the small basement, which was dominated by two safes. Many times he had supervised clerks putting things in, or taking things out, and never once had a mistake occurred. The basement gave Gregory a sense of pride.

He found it harder to reminisce on the ground floor with the counter removed and everything disordered. However he could still tell where his post had been when he first worked at Holborn, and he closed his eyes and brought to mind as many of his customers as he could. He thought of his regulars – those who had preferred to be served by him – and he wondered how many of them were still living.

Gregory opened his eyes and went into the branch manager's office. He scanned the room with his torch, and he looked a little guiltily at the spot where the chair had been; but it could not be said that he had deprived anyone: and Gregory told himself he was being unreasonable.

Then his mind slipped back to the many meetings he had had in that room, and his attempts to interest his various managers in his work. Gregory thought that one consequence of his efficiency was that his efforts had been taken for granted. His managers hadn't appreciated the intricacies of the daily work of the branch, and had been sparing in their praise. 'Too many high-fliers flew through this room,' Gregory thought. He knew he wouldn't have been happy as the branch manager, nor in any other senior post. He was a low-flier. But therefore more easily brought down.

Closing the door behind him he left the manager's office, and went up the stairs to the first floor. He went into the main office, turned right and walked to the desk by the far window. Hilary had worked there when she hadn't been at the counter. He wondered what she was doing at that precise moment. He hoped she was alive, and quietly sleeping beside somebody loving and rich. He hoped she would wake up the next morning and be happy; though he also hoped she would think of him during the next day with fondness, and at least some regret: for he certainly had his regrets over leaving her.

Gregory stood looking ahead of him sightlessly, musing over his decision, and the happiness that had not been his to take. Then he noticed his torch was pointing at the window, and turned it hurriedly to the floor. 'But what does it matter, Gregory? If the police come you'll hear them – same as the builders.'

Gregory waved his torch to and fro; he made patterns on the ceiling, and played it with abandon on the windows. Then he thought he saw something move to his left, and swung about. It was April.

His mind went blank with terror, his body convulsed, and he dropped his torch. It fell on Hilary's desk, and its beam continued to point at his dead sister.

Gregory grasped the desk with both hands to save himself from falling. He tried to speak but his mouth and throat were rigid. Gregory could not even croak.

After a while he realised he was looking at his sister as she had appeared just before she died.

She was wearing a hospital smock, her face was withered, and her hair was grey and sparse.

April smiled at Gregory, and she pulled off her smock to reveal the ruins of a desirable body. She spoke quietly, 'Not Hilary – no Gregory, no – it's me you belong to.'

April held him in her gaze for a very long minute; then she turned, picked up her smock, and walked out of the office; and Gregory crumpled onto his knees. He retched over Hilary's chair; but nothing came out of his mouth except a trickle of saliva. And without thinking what he was doing Gregory wiped his face on the seat in front of him.

Sometime later he managed to get up, and make his way towards the door. He stopped short though in his fear, and stood baffled as to what he should do. He thought April might be waiting outside. Eventually he realised he had no choice but to go forward, and inched onto the landing. He pointed his torch left and right, and up and down the stairs; but she wasn't there.

Keeping his back to the wall Gregory went sideways step by step up to the landing above. He was convinced she would be in the office, and called out, 'April, April,' in a trembling voice. But there was no answer.

Gregory peeped round the corner of the outer room, then stepped in. Trying to watch both the door behind him and the one in front, he moved forward. 'April, April,' he called again.

He had left a candle burning on his desk and was frightened by the solitary flame. Even with the beam of his torch pointing directly at it, he found the flickering light ghostly.

Gregory willed himself in, and flung the beam of his torch into every corner. He looked in the kitchen, and with a face full of horror yanked open the toilet door. April wasn't there.

Gregory went back to the door on the landing and locked it. In desperate hope he pushed the light switch, and finding that the electricity was still off, lit every candle he had; and crammed them onto his desk and along the shelves. He found sixty burning candles less ghostly than one; but still he stood in the corner of his room, waiting for April to come at him again.

'You didn't see her, Gregory,' he said in his fear, 'you've just gone mad.'

'But you saw her shadow, Gregory, didn't you?' He asked himself, and he had to acknowledge the torch had cast a shadow behind April. But he didn't know if that made it more likely she was a ghost or not. If he had imagined his dead sister was there, why not her shadow? And he didn't know if ghosts had shadows. It seemed wrong.

As he stood in the corner yearning for the dawn to break, he told himself repeatedly that he was mad. Then he decided he had to do something to try and calm himself, and went warily into the outer office and started to barricade the door.

He thought though his efforts were futile against April, as he presumed she could walk through the door and desks. Indeed he worked in the expectation of a hand reaching out from the door to grab him; and of her appearing behind his back.

More than ever Gregory wanted to die. He wanted the builders to arrive and everything to finish. He even wanted the branch to be torn down.

'But what are you going to do, Gregory, if they don't arrive?' He couldn't answer himself, and he flinched in fear. He knew he couldn't endure being reprieved for a day every day: his mind would collapse, if it hadn't already.

'But are the builders real, Gregory? Or did you imagine the men who came last week?'

He clasped his head and sunk to the floor.

'I heard them!' he shouted.

'But you saw April,' came the quiet reply.

Gregory sobbed; then he screamed. He got to his feet and he ran to the window.

'Morning, come!' he bellowed into the night. He span round, but April wasn't there.

He retreated back to the corner, but was too weak to stand; and slid down the wall to the floor.

'Why not die now, Gregory? The noose is prepared. Why not? But if you do die, Gregory, will it be the end? April's dead and she's still here.'

Death had been Gregory's last hope and the suggestion appalled him. Particularly, as he soon deduced, if it wasn't the end for him and April, then it wouldn't be the end for others. Gregory saw himself as a ghost amongst ghosts: jostled and mocked for having committed suicide; and this he saw lasting for ever. He imagined himself being told every day of the pain some other ghost would have endured for even a few more minutes of life; and he imagined himself trying to justify his actions through eternity. 'Hell is other people, Gregory, it's true.'

Gregory saw every Londoner who ever lived enduring. He saw every crowd of the living permeated and surrounded by crowds of the dead. He saw every building surviving in some shadowy form: every London that ever was, was still present, and would be forever.

He ran to the window in panic. There was no ghostly throng in the street: indeed there was no one there at all. And the buildings he saw were the ones he had known for years.

Gregory looked along Holborn to the east, and he believed he could see the first hint of dawn. He did not take his eyes away from this faint blur of light; because with this hope came the fear that April was in the room behind him, and he did not dare to look at her again.

So Gregory remained with his face pressed to the glass, silhouetted against the window by his sixty candles. Even when the sun rose clear of the roofs Gregory remained still, and waited for the full light of day. And by the time dawn had become morning his candles were out, and his desk and shelves were covered by cold streams of wax.

Gregory did not intend to endure another night. He found his hammer and nails, and once more pinned the door to its frame. He washed his face in cold water, and returned to his post at the window.

At quarter-past-seven a man in calf high boots and a dusty tracksuit walked along Holborn. He crossed the road, stopped outside the branch, pulled a sandwich from his holdall, peeled off the plastic cover, and started to eat.

'They're real, Gregory, the builders are real!'

Five minutes later a second builder came, then a third; and a fourth and a fifth together. Though it was the fifth builder who studied a crossword – separating himself from his colleagues, and pondering over his paper with the aid of a series of hand rolled cigarettes. Absorbed in studying this man, Gregory paid only slight attention to the swelling crowd below him.

However at the sight of a weighty man in a grey tweed jacket and tie, the builder with the crossword put his paper away; thus preventing Gregory from knowing which crossword it was. He felt wounded by this, but had no time to dwell on his regret.

'Hello, Jim! Another day, another bank!' The man in the tweed jacket called out from across the road; and Gregory knew the moment of crisis was almost upon him.

He checked his barricade. Then he looked at his office. Gregory tried to imagine it as it had been when he worked there. Eight o'clock was his normal time of arrival, and he pictured the scene in his mind. The first hour in the office had always been the happiest of the day. Gregory closed his eyes and remembered what he had been: until the booming voice from the street brought him back to the present.

'Still, Gregory,' he consoled himself, 'it's the right place for the end.'

He went to the window, but stood well clear of the glass for the fear of being seen by the man in the tweed jacket. Gregory could easily imagine him in the country, digging up burrows with a spade. He could see him grabbing some creature in its broken lair, giving it a gleeful shake, then throwing it amongst his dogs and laughing.

Gregory had no doubt as to what the builders would do to him if he were caught alive. He was certain they would start by breaking his ankles with their sledge hammers; then perhaps they would break his knees. He thought the man with the crossword would plead for mercy, but he couldn't see what one man could do against twenty. The only help he could provide would be a quick coup de grace.

Then Gregory heard the front door open, and the empty tin bounce across the floor; and he realised he wasn't ready. He pulled off his jacket and tie, and struggled with the buttons of his new shirt. He had intended to strip to the waist, but he panicked when he heard the builders come up the stairs.

Gregory yanked open the collar of his shirt, then locked the inner office door. As he did so he heard a thump and a shout: 'Hello.' Then there was a louder thump.

He found himself with the keys to both office doors in his hand, whereas he had intended to leave the key to the outer office door stuck in the lock. Yet it was too late to return now, as the thumps had turned to blows.

Gregory sellotaped the inner door key in place; and started to climb onto the kitchen table. But he realised he had left the telephone wire he needed in one of the desks in the outer office.

He tried to pull the wire from his own telephone, but he couldn't manage it with his hands. He felt in his trouser pockets for his Swiss Army knife but it wasn't there; yet he found it after a frantic search of his jacket.

He cut off two yards of wire, and in his haste cut open two of his fingers; and got blood on his suit. He scrambled onto the kitchen table, nearly fell off backwards, and got blood on the wall.

Gregory put his head in the noose. He put his hands behind him, and wound the wire about his wrists. He heard a splintering of wood, and a shout of triumph from the landing. And he tried to picture Hilary, and for a few seconds succeeded, before she was driven from his mind by the ghostly image of April.

Uncertain as to his future Gregory stepped off the table. Yet he stepped more forward than down, and swung out and then back. He knocked the table over, and his legs kicked about in the air, dislodging large chunks of plaster from the wall, and badly scuffing his brogues.

Only slowly did he grow quiet. And his corpse was still swaying gently when a panel was knocked out of the inner door, and his lolling tongue and purple face were exposed to the curious gaze of the builders.